A NOTE TO PARENTS

When your children are ready to "step into reading," giving them the right books is as crucial as giving them the right food to eat. **Step into Reading Books** present exciting stories and information reinforced with lively, colorful illustrations that make learning to read fun, satisfying, and worthwhile. They are priced so that acquiring an entire library of them is affordable. And they are beginning readers with a difference—they're written on five levels.

Early Step into Reading Books are designed for brand-new readers, with large type and only one or two lines of very simple text per page. **Step 1 Books** feature the same easy-to-read type as the Early Step into Reading Books, but with more words per page. **Step 2 Books** are both longer and slightly more difficult, while **Step 3 Books** introduce readers to paragraphs and fully developed plot lines. **Step 4 Books** offer exciting nonfiction for the increasingly independent reader.

The grade levels assigned to the five steps—preschool through kindergarten for the Early Books, preschool through grade 1 for Step 1, grades 1 through 3 for Step 2, grades 2 through 3 for Step 3, and grades 2 through 4 for Step 4—are intended only as guides. Some children move through all five steps very rapidly; others climb the steps over a period of several years. Either way, these books will help your child "step into reading" in style!

apple   balloons   bee   carrots   eyes

frog   house   love   mole   moon

mouse   nose   pie   pineapple   pizza

roses   sun   tie   toes

Text copyright © 2000 by Rita Golden Gelman.
Illustrations copyright © 2000 by Holly Hannon. All rights reserved under
International and Pan-American Copyright Conventions. Published in the
United States by Random House, Inc., New York, and simultaneously in
Canada by Random House of Canada Limited, Toronto.

www.randomhouse.com/kids

Library of Congress Cataloging-in-Publication Data
Gelman, Rita Golden.
Mole in a hole / by Rita Golden Gelman ; illustrated by Holly Hannon.
p. cm. — (Step into reading. A step 1 book)
SUMMARY: A lonely mole's animal friends find his hole too dark and small for them,
but in Ms. Mole he meets the perfect companion to share his life. Features rebuses
throughout the text.   ISBN 0-679-89037-8 (trade) — ISBN 0-679-99037-2 (lib. bdg.)
1. Rebuses. [1. Moles (Animals)—Fiction. 2. Animals—Fiction. 3. Stories in rhyme.
4. Rebuses.] I. Hannon, Holly, ill. II. Title. III. Series: Step into Reading.
Step 1 book. PZ8.3.G28Mm 2000 [E]—dc21 98-53770

Printed in the United States of America May 2000 10 9 8 7 6 5 4 3 2 1

Step into Reading®

Mole in a Hole

by Rita Golden Gelman
illustrated by Holly Hannon

A Step 1 Book

Random House 🏠 New York

There once was a
who lived in a hole
under an 🍎 tree.
Poor little
was lonely
as only a can be.

So he said to a  and a and a , "Come into my and eat with me."

"Sure," said the .

"Why not," said the .

"Okay," said the .

There were 4 in the .

But the  could not see.
He kept bumping his knee.
And the  tried to sit,
but she sat in her tea.

The  kept buzzing
and bumping her head.
"My feelers are broken,"
the little  said.

"Please eat,"
said the .
"I have .
I have stew.

I have  and ![carrots],
and ![pineapple], too."

11

"No, thanks," said the
and the
and the .

"How can we eat
if we cannot see?"

"I must go,"
said the ,
rubbing his knee.
"This hole is too dark
and too crowded for me."

The  hopped out.

And then there were 3.

"I cannot see my tail.

I am standing in stew.

Good-bye," said the .

And then there were 2.

16

"Well, how about me?"
said the sad little  .

"My visit is done."

And then there was 1.

The 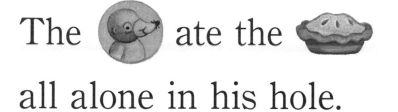 ate the all alone in his hole.

Then he packed up
some  and went for a stroll.

The 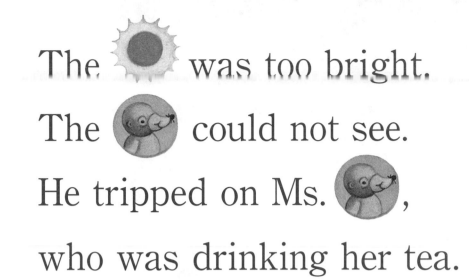 was too bright.

The could not see.

He tripped on Ms. ,

who was drinking her tea.

"I am sorry, Ms. .

Are you all right?"

"No, I am not!

That is too bright.

It hurts my 👁 👁.

It burns my 👃.

It dries my fur

and curls my 🦶."

"I cannot read.

I cannot write.

I hate the ☀.

I hate the light."

"Me too!" said the .

It was ♥ at first sight.

They wiggled their 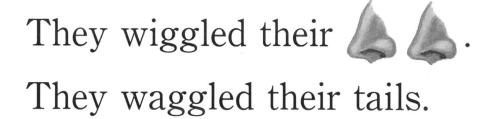.

They waggled their tails.

They talked about worms
and lizards
and snails.

They ate all the 🥕.

They sang out of tune.

Together they walked

by the light of the 🌙.

The wedding was set

for the first night in June.

The bride carried .

The groom wore a .

The  sang a song,

and the  brought the .

The 🎈 and the flowers
were done by the 🐭.

And the very next spring,

there were 6 in the .